The Purple Snerd

Rozanne Lanczak Williams
Illustrated by Mary GrandPré

Green Light Readers
Harcourt, Inc.
Orlando Austin New York
San Diego London

One morning in March,
Fern was sitting outside.
Then all of a sudden . . .
"*Snort! Chirp!*" something cried.

It was under the porch.
Who or what could it be?
Some long purple fur
was all Fern could see.

The Purple Snerd

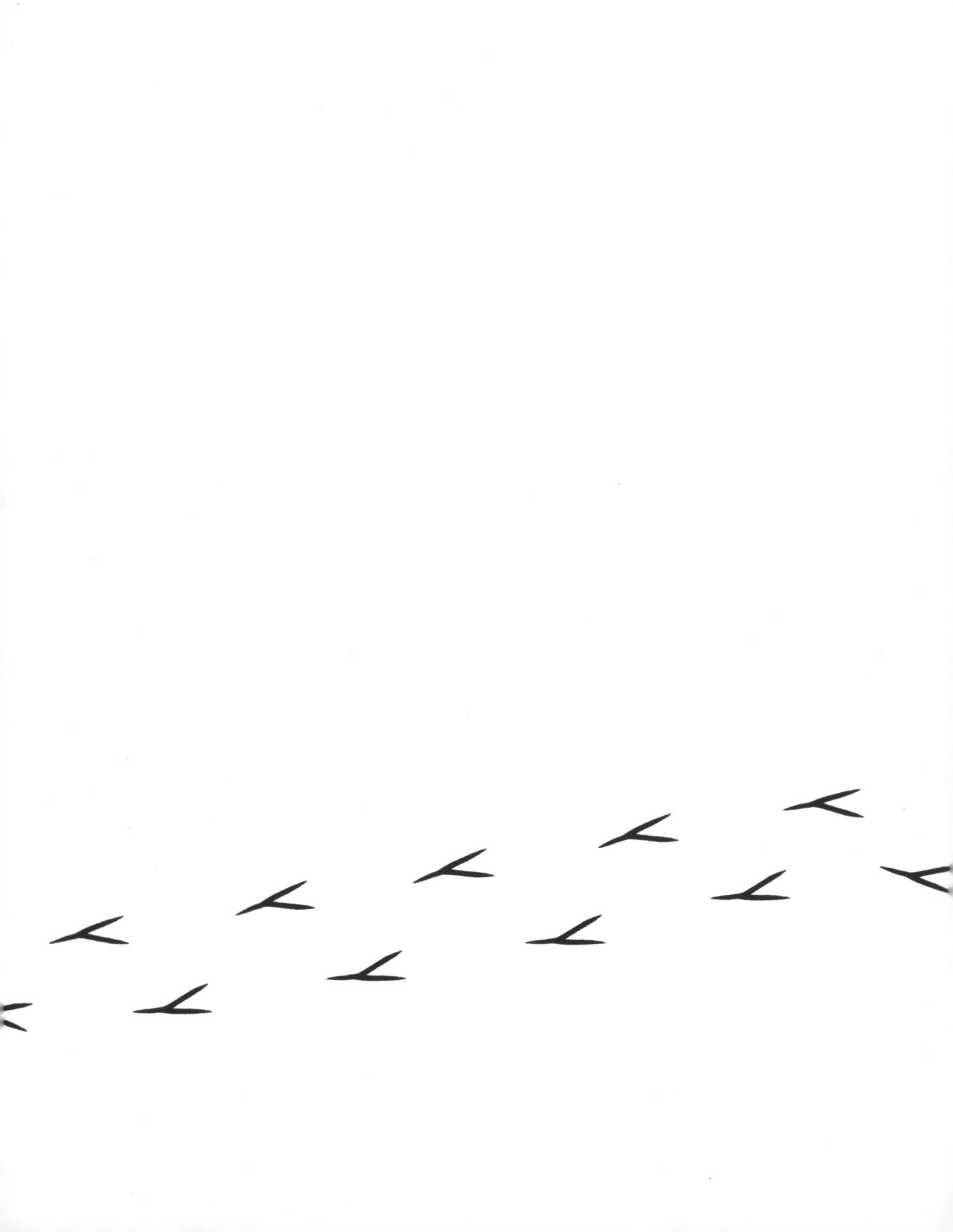

It was smaller than her horse.
It was bigger than a bird.
Fern couldn't believe it—
could this be a Snerd?

The first thing Fern did
was to open her book.
Then she sat on a step
and had a good look.

Purple Snerds, the book said,
will purr, bark, and chirp.
When they eat all their sweet snacks,
they will snort and slurp.

Curled under Fern's porch,
the thing chirped, barked, and purred.
It snorted and slurped
like a Purple Snerd!

It said, “Hello, Fern!
I’m so glad we’ve met!
Can you find some sweet snacks—
as sweet as they get?”

"You *are* a Snerd!" cried Fern.
"Big and purple, I see!
I saw Snerds in my book
and now one's here with me!"

Fern and the Snerd
played around and had fun.
They even played Snerdball
outside in the sun.

Their time went by fast,
and the Snerd had to go.
“So long, Fern,” he chirped.
“I’ll come back, you know.”

"So long," called Fern.
"It was such a fun day.
Bring more Purple Snerds
to my house to play!"

ACTIVITY

See what happens when you mix colors together.

WHAT YOU'LL NEED

paper

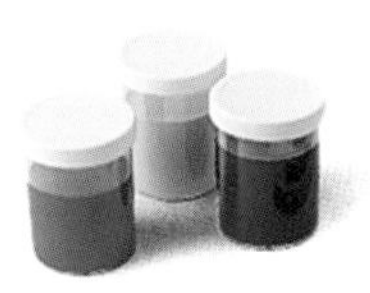

paints

paintbrush

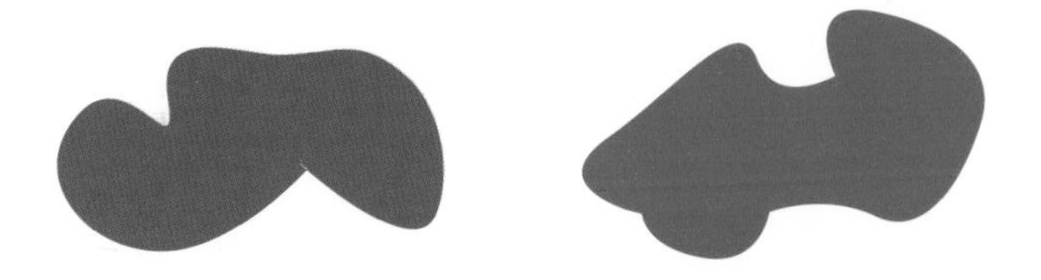

1. Mix blue and red together.
What new color do you get?

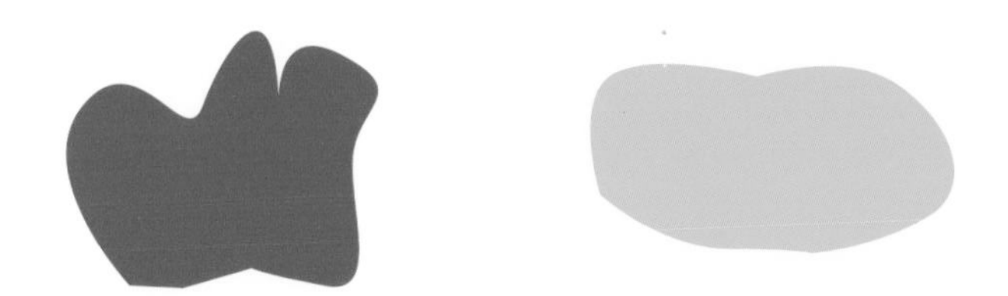

2. Mix red and yellow together.
What new color do you get?

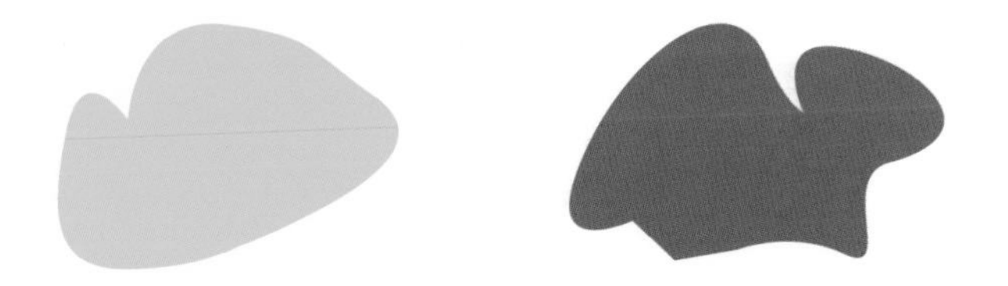

3. Mix yellow and blue together.
What new color do you get?

Which new color is your favorite?

ACTIVITY

Write a Story

Fern had a book about the Purple Snerd. Write a story about a character that is your favorite new color!

WHAT YOU'LL NEED

paper

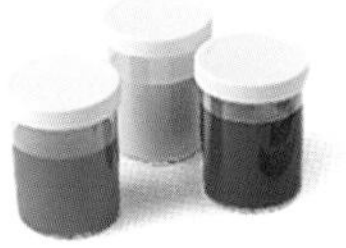

paints

paintbrush

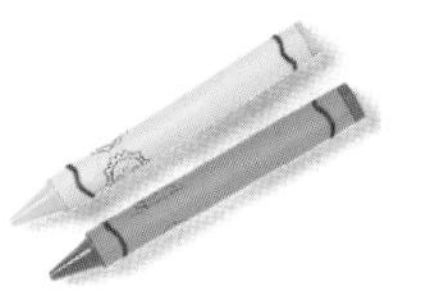

crayons or markers

1. Mix two colors to make your favorite new color.

2. Paint a character using that color. Name it when you're finished.

3. Write a story about your new character.

4. Share your picture and your story with a friend!

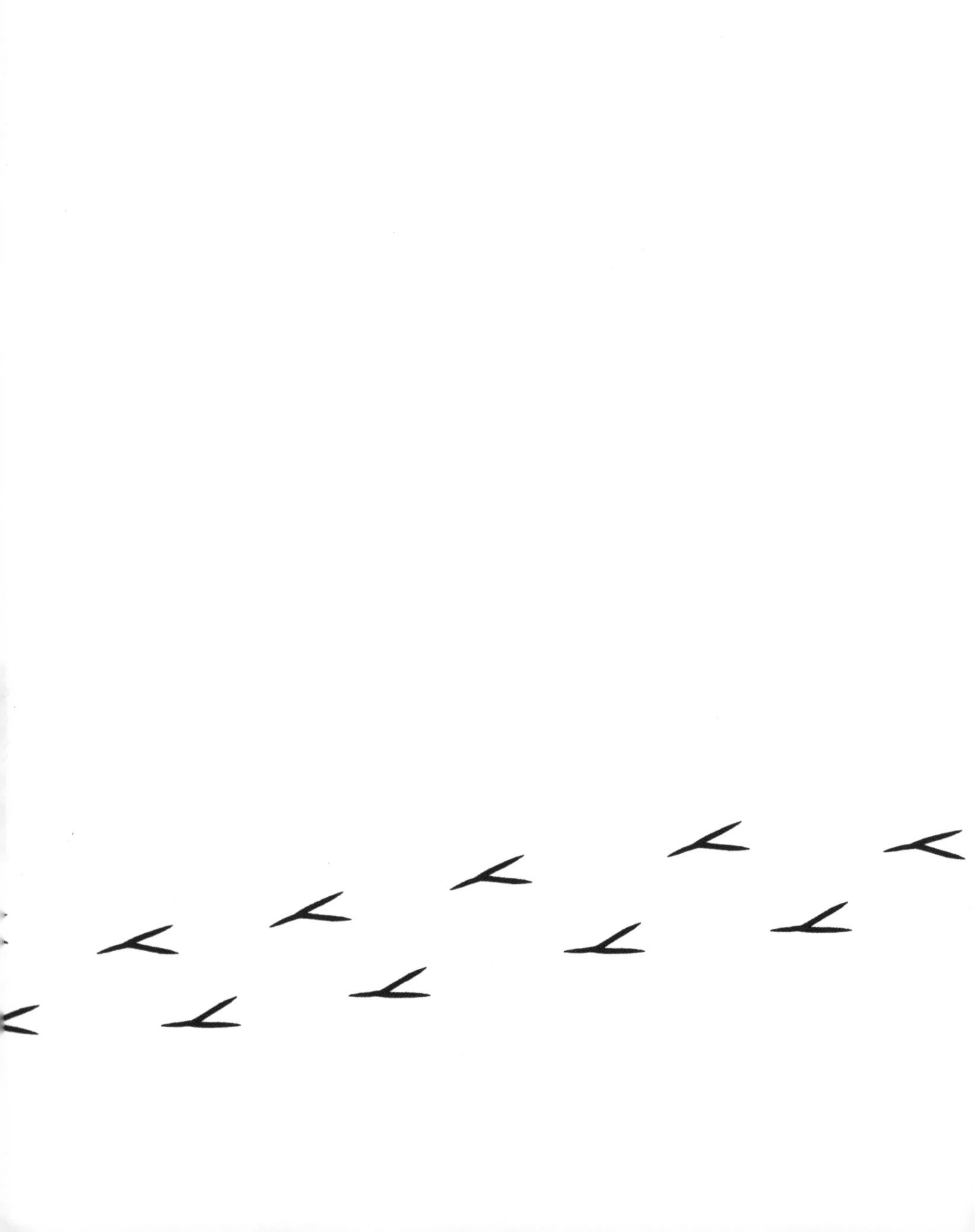

Meet the Illustrator

Mike Woodside

Mary GrandPré kept thinking of her dog, Charlie, when she tried to draw the Purple Snerd. Charlie has a hairy face and loves to eat sweets. Somehow, the Purple Snerd turned out to look a lot like Charlie! Besides drawing, Mary likes to visit schools. She tells children about her work and shows them how to draw, too.

Mary GrandPré

For information about permission to reproduce selections from this book, please write to Permissions, Houghton Mifflin Harcourt Publishing Company 215 Park Avenue South NY NY 10003

www.hmhco.com

First Green Light Readers edition 2000
Green Light Readers is a trademark of Harcourt, Inc., registered in the United States of America and/or other jurisdictions.

The Library of Congress has cataloged an earlier edition as follows:
Williams, Rozanne Lanczak.
The purple snerd/Rozanne Lanczak Williams; illustrated by Mary GrandPré.
p. cm.
"Green Light Readers."
Summary: When an imaginary creature appears under the porch, Fern looks in her book to determine its name, decides it's a purple snerd, and spends the day playing with it.
[1. Imaginary playmates—Fiction. 2. Stories in rhyme.]
1. GrandPré, Mary, ill. II. Title.
PZ8.3.W67926Pu 2000
[E]—dc21 99-50810
ISBN 978-0-15-204866-2
ISBN 978-0-15-204826-6 (pb)

SCP 12 11 10 9 8 7
4500524632

Ages 5–7

Grades: 1–2

Guided Reading Level: G–I

Reading Recovery Level: 15–16

"A must-have for any family with a beginning reader."—*Boston Sunday Herald*

"You can't go wrong with adding several copies of these terrific books to your beginning-to-read collection."—*School Library Journal*

"A winner for the beginner."—*Booklist*

Five Tips to Help Your Child Become a Great Reader

1. Get involved. Reading aloud to and with your child is just as important as encouraging your child to read independently.

2. Be curious. Ask questions about what your child is reading.

3. Make reading fun. Allow your child to pick books on subjects that interest her or him.

4. Words are everywhere—not just in books. Practice reading signs, packages, and cereal boxes with your child.

5. Set a good example. Make sure your child sees YOU reading.

Why Green Light Readers Is the Best Series for Your New Reader

- Created exclusively for beginning readers by some of the biggest and brightest names in children's books

- Reinforces the reading skills your child is learning in school

- Encourages children to read—and finish—books by themselves

- Offers extra enrichment through fun, age-appropriate activities unique to each story

- Incorporates characteristics of the Reading Recovery program used by educators

- Developed with Harcourt School Publishers and credentialed educational consultants